Catch My Kiss

Copyright © 2019 by Kimberly DiVita Smith

Illustrations & Page Layout by Heather Workman

All rights reserved.

ISBN: 978-0-578-51211-2

Library of Congress Control Number: 2019905293

Kimberly DiVita Smith

www.booksbykds.com

Catch
My Kiss

By Kimberly DiVita Smith

Illustrated by Heather Workman

For Charlotte & Emelia,
Forever catching my kisses.

Each day I see your face,
my love could leave a trace;
and follow you around
without making any sound.

Wherever today takes you,
know you're on my mind.
Close your eyes and think of me -
I won't be hard to find.

Because you're a part of me,
and I'm a part of you...
So wherever you may be,
a piece of me will be there too!

Now listen closely to these words
and hold them in your heart -
I am always with you
and have been from the start.

Catch my kiss and don't you miss!
Every day is such a gift.
No matter what is on my list,
my heart is full with you in it!

Some days go by oh so fast!
You have school, you have soccer -
you even have dance class!
Tell me what you've learned today -
did you have a blast?!

I won't grow tired of hearing your stories,
especially when they end in moments of glory.
And as you share with so much care,
I have a hunch I must pack lunch!

For tomorrow is another day,
with a new adventure on its way.
You'll teach me something I don't know
and remind me how lucky I am
to get to watch you grow.

With the start of this new day,
remember what I say...

Catch my kiss and don't you miss!
Every day is such a gift.
Be good, be confident and always be kind,
and happiness you'll surely find.

In moments I can't be by your side,
know I'm here for the forever ride.
Over every bump and through every turn,
there is just so much that we will learn.

I'll have your back
and give no slack,
while you learn to hustle
and flex those muscles!
Aim for great—cooperate.
I'll see you tonight - we'll make it a date!

But for now,
catch my kiss and don't you miss!
Every day is such a gift.

I'll catch yours too,
wink back at you,
saying "Have a great day!"
as I go on my way.

My day may be filled with meetings and calls,
but you will always be the center of it all.
I do it for you and I do it for me,
to show us both we can be what we dream to be.

Before I know it,
I look at the time -
I'm homeward bound
and feeling just fine.

My favorite part of the day is here!
I'm home and get to hold you near.
You help me stay humble,
both feet on the ground.
My life is complete when you are around.

Now it's time we tuck into bed
and talk briefly about the book we just read.
Before saying goodnight and hugging you tight,
always remember what I have said...

Catch my kiss and don't you miss!
Every day is such a gift.
Now go to sleep, I insist!

CPSIA information can be obtained
at www.ICGtesting.com
Printed in the USA
BVHW09002224Q0619
551756BV00002BA/4/P